MOSES SUPPOSES HIS TOESES ARE ROSES
ARE ROSES
And 7 Other Silly Old Rhymes

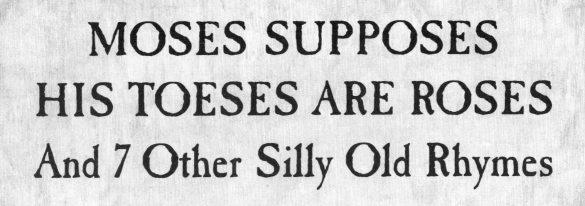

MOSES SUPPOSES
HIS TOESES ARE ROSES
And 7 Other Silly Old Rhymes

RETOLD AND ILLUSTRATED BY

Nancy Patz

HBJ

A VOYAGER/HBJ BOOK

HARCOURT BRACE JOVANOVICH, PUBLISHERS

SAN DIEGO   NEW YORK   LONDON

Also by Nancy Patz

GINA FARINA AND THE PRINCE OF MINTZ

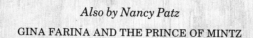

Requests for permission to make copies of any part
of the work should be mailed to:
Copyrights and Permissions Department,
Harcourt Brace Jovanovich, Publishers,
Orlando, Florida 32887.

Printed and bound by South China Printing Company, Hong Kong

LIBRARY OF CONGRESS CATALOGING IN PUBLICATION DATA
Patz, Nancy. Moses supposes his toeses are roses and 7 other silly old rhymes.
SUMMARY: Includes "Algie and the Bear," "The Tooter," and "Dizzy McPete."
1. Nursery rhymes.   [1. Nursery rhymes]   I. Title.
PZ8.3.P27364Mo 1983   398'.8   82-3099
ISBN 0-15-255691-5 (pbk.)

A B C D E F

To my father, Harry J. Patz

BETTY BOTTER

Betty Botter bought some butter.
"But," she said, "the butter's bitter!
If I put it in my batter,
It will make my batter bitter.

"But a bit of better butter—
That will make my batter better!"

So she bought a bit of butter—
Better than her bitter butter—

And she put it in her batter,
And her batter wasn't bitter.

Wasn't it better Betty Botter
Bought a bit of better butter?

Bet your bonnet,
Betty Botter!

SWEETIE  MAGUIRE

"FIRE! FIRE!"
said Sweetie Maguire.

"Where? Where?"
said Mrs. O'Hair.

"Down the street!"
said Teenie-Feet.

"Get some water!"
said her daughter.

"Jump! Jump!"
said Mr. Plump.

"Don't be silly!"
said Willy-Nilly.

"What's in the
cupboard?" said
Old Pa Hubbard.

"A squishy fish,"
said Lickitty-Dish.

"Is that all?"
said Mr. Ball.

"And enough, too!"
said Mrs. Chew.
And . . .

away
they
flew!

Away
they
flew!

DIZZY McPETE

A fellow named Dizzy McPete
Is always exceedingly neat.
When he gets out of bed,
He stands on his head
To be sure he won't dirty his feet!

Neat!

ALGIE AND THE BEAR

Algie met a bear.
The bear met Algie.

The bear was bulgy.
The bulge was Algie.

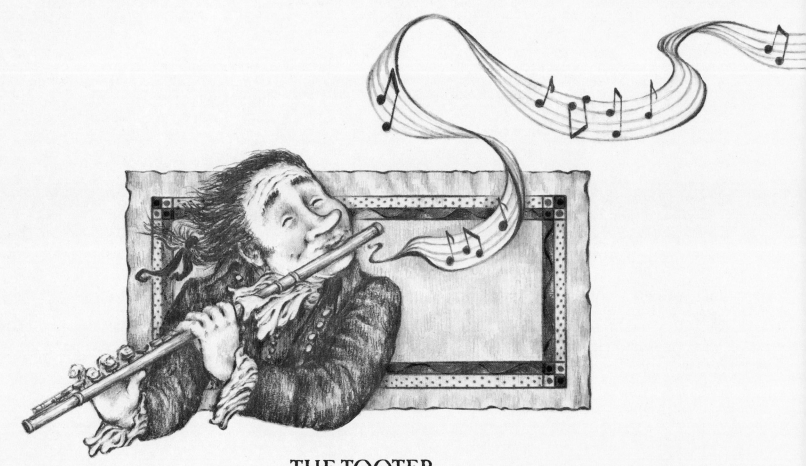

THE TOOTER

A tooter who tooted the flute
  Tried to tutor two tooters to toot.
"Toot-toot!" said the tooters.
"Tut-tut!" said the tutor.
"It's harder to tutor . . .

. . . than toot!"
So he tooted to Kalamazoo,
Where he dreamt he was eating a shoe.

He awoke in the night
With a terrible fright
And found it was perfectly true!

Cuckoo!

MARY AND HER LITTLE LAMB

Mary had a little lamb.
It was a greedy glutton.

She fed it ice cream all day long
And now it's frozen mutton.

ESAU AND KATE

MOSES AND HIS TOESES

Moses
supposes
his toeses
are roses,

But Moses supposes erroneously,

For nobody's toeses we knowses are roses,

As Moses
supposes
his toeses
to be!